Mr. Brown, Sadie, and Me

This book is dedicated to my grandkids, Vince, Ava, Angelo, and Cam and to all kids who are afraid to pick up dog poop! I am grateful to two young girls who helped me critique this book; Olive and Moxie! They were fun to work with.

I wonder, are other kids ever scared of old people? Well, here's my story.

My name is Brian. Where I live, there are many kinds of people, some old and some young. I hang out only with kids. Mom and I go for a walk most every day. I used to have to hold her hand, but now that I'm 8, I don't have to do that anymore!

Sadie

We see lots of crazy stuff on our walks. I saw
an old man who was trying to walk his dog. The
dog was being hyper, the man was barely moving.
My mom said hello and introduced us. His name
was Mr. Brown and he put out his hand to me.
I guess I was suppose to shake it, so I did. But
I couldn't look at him. I felt kinda nervous.

I liked the dog though, she was pretty cute.

I said, "Can we help you with your dog?"
That was pretty bold of me!

"Oh yes," he smiled "that would very helpful! Her name is Sadie and she has a lot more energy than I do. It's getting harder to walk her. I live right there in the yellow house." He pointed, then he handed mom the leash and a little bag, "You might need this if she has to, well you know what!"

She took the leash then turned to me and whispered, "Go on Brian, take his hand and help him to his door." I felt stuck!

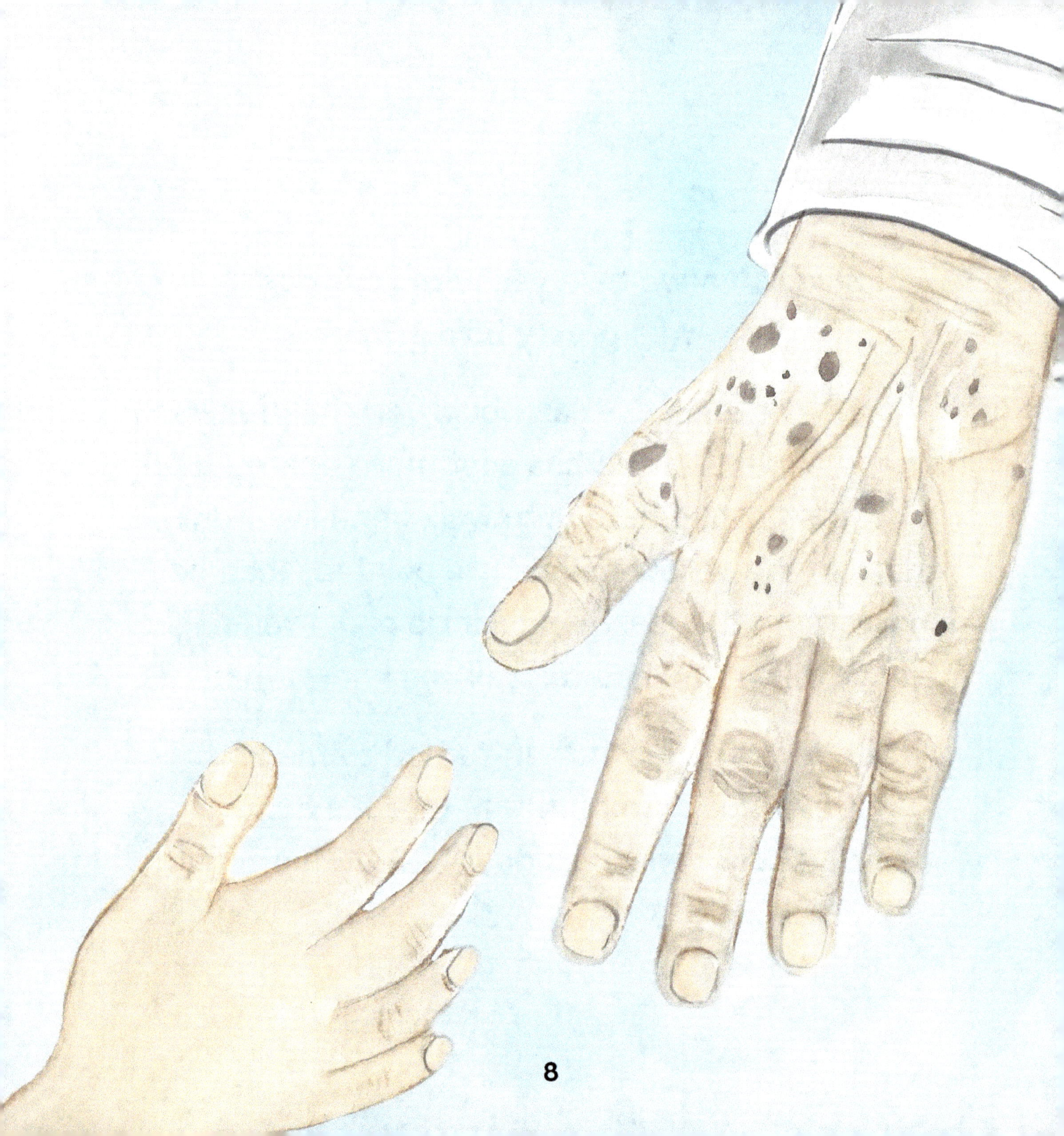

I looked at Mr. Brown's hand. It was all wrinkly with bumps and spots all over. It felt cold and a lot different than mom or dad's. I felt it shaking a little too.

Maybe he was just as nervous as me. I've never touched someone that old before.

Sadie
Werther's Original

It took a LONG time to get to his door. I
was wondering, 'does everyone walk this
slow when they get old?' As soon as he
opened the door, I wanted to bolt...

"Wait!" he said, "I have something for you." He
handed me a little candy with gold foil. "Thanks"
and I ran off before he could say another word.

Mom smiled, "Thanks Brian, when people get that old, they need all the help and kindness they can get."

I had so many questions for her, "Why does he go so slow? Why was his hand cold? Are all old people shaky?"

"Well....people age differently," she said. "My guess is that he's in his 90's and maybe has some health issues that hurt when he moves."

So we continued walking Sadie who wanted to smell EVERYTHING in the WORLD! But she really was the cutest dog I've ever seen!

"Here, you take her back to Mr. Brown." She handed me Sadie's leash. I rang his doorbell and knocked. Seemed like I waited forever. He finally came. He held on to the wall while he opened the door. (Was he sick?)

I handed him Sadie's leash. "Thank you." he said in a scratchy voice.

Werther's Original
Sadie

The next day I suggested we stop at Mr. Brown's
to see if we could help walk Sadie. He came
slowly to the door. Sadie was so happy. Her
tail was wagging really hard, it nearly knocked
Mr. Brown over. I guess she knew us already.
He gave us the leash and another bag.

When we returned, Mr. Brown was sitting
on the porch swing. Mom and I both came
up and again he gave us a candy. It was
butterscotch and I liked it a lot!.

Sadie

Every day we stopped at his house to get Sadie.
And every day he gave us a butterscotch.

One day he said, "You know I've been thinking,
would you like a job? I would pay you $2 a
day.?" He looked at me... I looked at Mom.

'Me?' I thought, 'I WILL be 9 soon.
That would be kinda cool!'

"What do you have in mind, Mr. Brown?" Mom asked.

"Well," he said, "Sadie has lots of energy. Could
he walk her after school around 4 o'Clock?"

"Hmmm, Brian is pretty young." She told him she
would think about it and let him know tomorrow.

STAR
WARS

That night Mom and Dad both talked to me. They talked about the responsibility of walking a dog and going to Mr. Brown's house every day. They said I would have to walk the same way everyday and stay on the sidewalk to be safe. Then Dad added, "You know Brian, if the dog poops, you will have to pick it up." YUCK, that sounded awful. "Is that what that little blue bag was for? I wouldn't like doing THAT."

Mom nodded, "That would be part of the job, you must promise to be responsible," Hmmmmm, maybe I could figure out how to pick it up without touching the "you know what."

I'm thinking, 'I DO like being with Sadie and I would like $2 a day to buy stuff.' "OK," I said proudly, "I'll do it!"

Dog Bag

Mom told Mr. Brown I could start the next day. So I practiced picking up a tennis ball with a dog bag. I slip my hand inside all the way to the bottom, grab it, hold it tight and pull it through. The tennis ball kept dropping, but after a few dozen tries, I got it. After you grab it, you pull it through, it turns the bag kinda inside out (that's the tricky part), then twist it closed. I practiced grabbing different stuff; a rag, a Hot Wheel and even a Kleenex.

So finally, I told myself "You Got this!"

Sadie
26

The next day I went all by myself to Mr. Brown's. He came to the door a little quicker today. He had Sadie all ready to go. I was pretty nervous going around the block the first time alone. But I saw Mom and Ava, my 4 year old sister, watching me from the corner. I said to myself, 'I can handle this!'

When I got back to his house,
Mr. Brown was smiling.

The walks were going pretty good. I even liked
seeing Mr. Brown. Sometimes we would sit on the
porch and eat cookies. He was easy to talk to, not
like mom and dad who ask a billion questions. He just
listened and hummed and nodded once in a while.

Dog Bag

One walk was kinda weird. Sadie was walking just fine, then suddenly she stopped. She started circling around and around and then "OH NO, she's pooping!" Right on the sidewalk.

I wanted to run away but a promise is a promise. So I got out the bag, opened it up, put my hand all the way to the bottom and took a deep breath! It was NOT like the tennis ball! It felt soft and warm and squishy! I quickly turned it inside out and held my breath as I twisted it as fast as I could.

We ran back to Mr. Brown's. "This is from Sadie," I blurted out.

"Well, Brian, you're a real dog walker now!" He chuckled. "That deserves 2 butterscotches".

Sadie

The more I helped Mr. Brown with Sadie, the more I liked them both. He's kinda a smart guy for being as old as he is. I saw him do a really hard cross-word puzzle and he's trying to teach me Chess. He doesn't hear me all the time, but I'm learning to talk louder.

He showed me some of his baseball cards. These are from "the good ole days" he said proudly. "Can it be a 'good ole day' today?" I asked. He just smiled and handed me 2 butterscotches. Yep, I think I am going to like spending time with him.

You know, I'm going tell all my friends that old people are nothing to be scared of. They can even be fun.

Author's Note:

I wrote this book for 2 purposes; One; to illuminate the value of kids getting to know elderly people and learning to communicate with them. Two: to help kids ages 6-10 develop some independence and responsibility. The dog poop part adds some reality and humor to the book. It can be read individually or with a group of kids anywhere from 5-9 years old.

www.ingramcontent.com/pod-product-compliance
Lightning Source LLC
Chambersburg PA
CBHW080603300726
48975CB00010B/2775